ANIMAL
RESCUE CENTER

The Home-alone Kitten

ANIMAL MAGIC

This series is for my riding friend Shelley,
who cares about all animals.

tiger tales

5 River Road, Suite 128, Wilton, CT 06897
Published in the United States 2016
Originally published in Great Britain 2006
by Little Tiger Press
Text copyright © 2006, 2016 Jenny Oldfield
Interior illustrations copyright © 2016 Artful Doodlers
Cover illustration copyright © 2016 Anna Chernyshova
Images courtesy of www.shutterstock.com
ISBN-13: 978-1-58925-493-0
ISBN-10: 1-58925-493-7
Printed in China
STP/1800/0097/0216
10 9 8 7 6 5 4 3 2 1

For more insight and activities, visit us at www.tigertalesbooks.com

ANIMAL
RESCUE CENTER

The Home-alone Kitten

by TINA NOLAN

tiger tales

ANIMAL MAGIC
RESCUE CENTER

🏠 HOME

🐾 ADOPT

✋ FRIENDS

MEET THE ANIMALS IN NEED OF A HOME!

APACHE

7-year-old piebald, 13.1 hands, Apache is looking for a clever rider who will take him out in company or alone.

MARSHMALLOW

We don't know Marshmallow's age, and she won't look her best until her clipped fur grows back ... but she'll love you to pieces!

PEPPER

A two-year-old border collie cross with tons of energy. Can you play ball with her and give her all the walks she needs?

SITE SEARCH

 NEWS

 **HELP US**

 **CONTACT**

 DONATE!

SATIN

A beautiful 5-year-old Siamese who would like you to pamper her. She needs to be an only pet.

BECKETT

A 4-year-old great dane and a friendly giant! He needs a very special home with plenty of room to stretch his legs.

KITTENS

One adorable litter is 10 weeks old. You'll fall in love with Candy, Pixie, and Snap the moment you see them!

Chapter One

"'Animal Magic—we match the perfect pet with the pefect owner!'"

Ella Harrison read the words on the computer screen. "You forgot the 'r' in the second 'Perfect,'" she pointed out to her brother, Caleb. They'd been working together for almost an hour, designing a flier for Animal Magic's anniversary celebration.

Caleb added the "r" and scrolled through the rest of the flier. "Can I print it now?" he asked.

"Just a minute." Ella read the entire thing one last time. "'We take in and care for unwanted animals and find homes for them with caring owners.' Yep, cool. 'We make sure that no healthy animal is ever put to sleep.' Yeah, that's good. 'In our first year we placed 124 dogs and 156 cats in new homes. We also found new owners for 5 horses and 2 goats, plus 42 rabbits and 13 guinea pigs.'" She looked at the photos underneath. There was one of three feral kittens, Candy, Pixie, and Snap, and another of a white rabbit named Pom-Pom. "Cute!" she said.

"So can I print it?" Caleb asked impatiently.

"Wait!" Ella read on. "'Animal Magic's Anniversary Celebration.

Saturday, August 5. Meet a celebrity!'
This is the best part! 'Soccer star Jake
Adams will be here to greet fans at 2:00
p.m. Jake and his girlfriend, Marietta,
are big fans of Animal Magic, so don't
miss your chance to chat and get Jake's
autograph!' Can you believe it!"

"I know, this really is cool!" Caleb
agreed, tapping keys to begin printing
the fliers. He and his best friend,
George, were seriously into soccer.
"I can't wait to meet Jake!"

"I already have," Ella reminded him.
It wasn't often that she had one up on
her older brother, but this time she did.
"I was with Dad when he took Charlie
to Jake's house, remember?"

"Yeah, no need to rub it in," Caleb
muttered, keeping an eye on the printer

as it churned out the fliers.

Ella sailed on regardless. "Jake lives at Crystal Park Manor, an enormous mansion with a swimming pool. He came to the door with Marietta. I handed him Charlie and he said thanks. He said we were doing a great job."

"Yeah, yeah!" Caleb sniffed. "Next you'll be telling me that it was you who persuaded him to come to our event!"

"Yeah, well, no, actually, that was Dad." Ella had to admit the truth. "Jake invited us in. That was when Dad asked him to be our last-minute celebrity guest. Jake said yes, he'd love to do it if it helps to raise our pro-feel—"

"Raise our what?" Caleb cut in.

"Pro-feel—y'know, if it helps make us more well known."

"You mean profile!" Caleb grinned.

"Whatever." Taking a stack of fliers fresh from the printer, Ella blushed and made a quick exit. "Only two days to go!" she muttered. "I'd better pass these out, and put them up all over town."

"Here, take another *peel!*" Caleb laughed. "And remember, take it easy— delivering those fliers means you'll have to walk *meels* and *meels!*"

"Ha!" Ella retorted, flouncing off to the animal clinic to find their mom.

"Hi, Dad. Is Mom here?" Ella asked, popping her head around the office door. "Is she in the clinic?"

Her dad looked up from his pile of papers. "She's in the stables, vaccinating the two ponies we brought in yesterday."

Ella hurried past the operating room and the row of converted barns that housed the smaller rescue animals until she came to the small block of new stables that her dad had been working on for the last few weeks. "Mom?" she called, stepping out of the sunlight into the stables.

"Shh!" her mom, Heidi, whispered. She was petting the neck of a small

brown-and-white pony whose shaggy
mane fell over his dark eyes. "Apache
didn't like his injection, did you, boy?"

"Oh! But it'll make you feel better,"
said Ella, scratching Apache's nose.
Quietly, she went up to the other pony,
a skinny chestnut named Rosie. "Do you
want to be petted, too?" she whispered.

Rosie nuzzled Ella's palm with her soft nose. Inside the stall, a hay-net hung from the wall, and there was a bucket of feed on the floor.

"We'll soon fix you up and make you big and strong!" Ella promised, remembering the parched field where they had found her. A neighbor had called Animal Magic to say that the poor creature had been left without fresh water and abandoned by her owners while they took a two-week vacation in California.

"Hey, Apache," her mom whispered, still petting the little piebald. "Now that needle didn't really hurt, did it?" She turned to Ella. "Did you want something?" she reminded her.

"Oh, yeah. We finished the fliers

14

about the anniversary celebration.
I wanted to ask if I can deliver them
around town."

"Let me see."

Ella handed her mom a flier. Mom
read through it, nodding and finally
saying, "Yes, that's fine. It looks very
good…. Ella, did you hear me?"

"Hmm?" Ella had her arms around
Rosie's neck and she was whispering
sweetly into the pony's ear. "Oh, yeah.
Thanks, Mom!"

Mom smiled. "Go!" she urged.

"Okay, I'm out of here!" Ella said.
"Here I come, Crystal Park!"

Chapter Two

Ella hurried up Main Street, putting fliers into mailboxes, humming as she went. She felt really excited about Saturday. All the plans were going well, especially since Jake Adams had agreed to be there.

"Hi, George. Are you coming on Saturday?" she called to Caleb's best friend, who stood next to his bike in his driveway. She waved a flier in front of his face. "You'll get to meet Jake Adams if you do!"

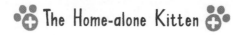

"Wow, no way! Seriously?"

Ella nodded. "So you'll come?" She was already moving onto the next house.

"Count me in," George said. He rode after Ella to the house next door. "What time will Jake be there?"

"Two o'clock!" she called over her shoulder. "But get there early if you want his autograph!"

"Our big day will be here soon!" Ella told Candy, Snap, and Pixie, one of four litters of kittens at Animal Magic. Charlie was their brother, and so far, he was the only one to have found a perfect new home.

"We'll have to make you look extra

handsome on Saturday," she cooed, lifting out 10-week-old Snap and tickling his tummy.

The brown tabby wriggled and squirmed.

"Yes, I know, you're already adorable!" Ella laughed. Her dad had found the litter in an air vent at the back of a factory. Realizing that they were wild, and seemingly without their mom, he had brought them back to Animal Magic. Ella had given the four kittens names before Jake Adams had come along and taken Charlie.

"There'll be hundreds of people," she promised, putting Snap back into his cage, then moving on to check on a Siamese stray named Satin. Right now, the cat unit was bursting at the seams with animals needing owners, just like the dog kennels next door.

"Hundreds of people!" Ella repeated, as she closed the door and went to the dog kennels to see Pepper, Bruno, and Beckett. "Down, Beckett!" she said sternly to the black great dane.

Beckett was almost as tall as Ella—a gentle giant who had been dumped at their doorstep a month earlier. He gazed at her with soft brown eyes that would melt the hardest heart.

"*Hundreds!*" she promised, going from one cage to the next.

The dogs woofed and whined. They jumped up and wagged their tails.

"People will line up for Jake Adams's autograph, and then they'll come to visit you," she told them. "They'll see you and fall in love with you. Before you know it, they'll want to take you home."

"Woof!" the dogs replied. "Woof— wruff—woof!"

Ella looked up at the pink sky as the sun disappeared in the west. "It's going to be the best, best day!"

Chapter Three

"Hi, Ella. Can I come in?" Annie Brooks poked her head around the door to the cat unit.

It was early Friday morning, and Ella was feeding the cats. "Sure. Why not?"

Annie bit her lip nervously. "I wondered if you were still talking to me, after what Mom and Dad have done."

Ella smiled. "We don't have a problem with you, Annie. Only your mom and dad!"

"I'm so sorry!" Annie sighed. She sidled up to the kitten area, where Candy, Snap, and Pixie snoozed in the warmth. "You know what Mom's like. She's always joining committees and setting up campaigns against stuff. Last year it was to stop cars speeding through town."

"And this year it's to close us down," said Ella. "But why doesn't she like us?" she asked, placing a bowl of food in front of a white cat named Marshmallow. Marshmallow's long coat had been so filthy and matted that Ella's mom had decided to shave it off, except for the fur on her face and tail. Now she looked strange and scrawny as she gobbled her food.

Annie shrugged. "She thinks you're noisy and attract too much traffic, stuff like that."

22

"Doesn't she care about animals?"

"Yes, she does. But she doesn't like having them next door, that's all." Annie wanted to change the subject, so she asked if she could pick up Pixie.

"Go ahead," Ella told her. "With any luck, by this time tomorrow, she might not be here!"

Annie nestled the tiny kitten against her. "So cute!" she muttered. Pixie meowed and cuddled up close. "Oh, have they found you a new home?"

"Not yet. But it's our anniversary celebration tomorrow, so here's hoping!"

23

Annie frowned and put Pixie back into the cage. She used her fingers to comb her dark hair behind her ears. "What celebration?"

"Oh," Ella said, feeling embarrassed. "Um, yeah—I was too scared to put a flier in your mailbox," Ella said. "I thought your mom might get angry with me. Anyway, we're inviting the entire town to Animal Magic so they can see what we do. Mom says it'll help find new owners for all the animals."

"Hmm." Annie's frown deepened. "That means lots of cars and lots of people. Maybe I'd better break it to Mom."

"Okay, if you think that's best," Ella said. "But poor you!"

"Yeah, I'd better go," Annie decided, heading for the door.

"Take a break," Ella's mom suggested when she saw Ella pushing a wheelbarrow toward the manure heap at the back of the yard. "Don't wear yourself out. It's going to be a long day."

"I'm fine!" Ella insisted. "I want to finish mucking out."

Her mom waited at the stable door until Ella came back with an empty wheelbarrow. "Good job!" She smiled. "I just came to take a look at Apache, to make sure he's okay after yesterday's jab."

"Apache's fine," Ella said, following Mom into the stables. "But take a look at Rosie. She's stomping around and pawing the ground. She doesn't look very happy."

Ella's mom nodded. She looked at the little chestnut mare, who had now gone down onto her knees and was trying to roll onto her side inside her stall. "This doesn't look good," Mom muttered, springing into action. "Ella, please get me a head collar. We need to get Rosie out of here and walking around the yard as quickly as possible."

Ella did as she was told. "What is it? What's wrong?" She held open the stable door as her mom buckled the head collar, got the pony back on her feet, and then led her outside.

"It could be colic," Mom replied. "If we've caught it early, she'll be okay."

Ella gasped and caught up with her mom. "And if not?" she asked.

"Colic is serious." Her mom didn't

hide the facts. "If we haven't gotten to her in time, I'm afraid Rosie could die!"

"Poor Rosie!" Caleb exclaimed. He had seen what was happening from the kitchen window and run out to help. He took over the lead-rope from Mom, who ran to get her vet's bag from the clinic.

Ella felt helpless as she watched the pony stiffen her legs and refuse to walk. Then Rosie turned her head toward her flank and curled her lip to show her teeth. "Mom, hurry. She looks like she's in real trouble!"

Her mom ran back. She checked Rosie's symptoms. "Yes, she's sweating, and her heart is racing. I'm pretty sure this is colic."

"Come on, girl," Caleb urged.

"It's probably due to her change of

diet," Mom told them. She pressed her hands against Rosie's flank. "Yes, it feels like there's some kind of intestinal blockage. But if we keep walking her, it might clear itself."

"Walk!" Ella begged.

"Yes. Come on, Rosie, you can do it!" Caleb urged.

Gamely the little pony responded to their voices. She took a step forward, then another. Gradually she began to move around the yard.

"Good work!" Mom told Caleb and Ella. In an emergency she always stayed calm. "Ella, keep talking to her. Caleb, keep some pressure on the rope to lead her on."

"Does it hurt a lot?" Ella asked Mom, who nodded. "It'll soon be better," Ella soothed.

"We hope!" Caleb muttered.

Walking ahead of Rosie, Ella checked over her shoulder to see that the pony was still following. Out of the corner of her eye, she noticed Linda Brooks appear at the main gate. "Uh-oh!" she warned the others. "Here comes more trouble!"

"Everything okay?" Ella's dad, Mark, asked Ella. He'd called home during his lunch break. "Are we all ready for the big day?"

"Um, actually not so good," Ella told him. "Rosie's got colic. Caleb and I are taking turns walking her around the yard."

"Oh, no. How is she?" Her dad sounded worried.

"A little better. Mom says it's probably a food blockage, so hopefully it's not going to be serious long-term. Her temperature's going down now."

"Good. What else?"

"Mrs. Brooks came around."

"Uh-oh!" Dad knew this could only

mean one thing. "What happened?"

"Annie told her about our anniversary celebration. Mrs. Brooks got really mad and yelled at Mom. Mom kept her cool and said she was busy with an emergency. Mrs. Brooks said she'd call the police if cars blocked her driveway. She stomped around, and then she went home."

"Oh, dear," Dad said. "Maybe I'll stop over and see them when I get home from work."

"One more thing," Ella added, to crown what had been a bad morning. "Caleb listened to the weather forecast and it's not good. There's supposed to be a thunderstorm tomorrow."

"Just what we need!" There was a long silence, and then her dad gave a deep sigh. "Oh, well. Maybe things aren't going according to plan," he said. "But at least we still have the appearance of Jake Adams up our sleeves!"

"Don't give Rosie anything to eat until I say so," Mom told Ella before heading off to the clinic. A stray dog had just been brought in by one of the Animal Magic volunteers, and it needed a full examination. "She can drink plenty of water, but no food!"

Ella nodded and stroked Rosie's nose. The sick pony was back in her stable, still shaking from the pain of her colic. But her temperature and pulse were back to normal. She was over the worst of it.

"Good girl!" Ella soothed as Rosie nuzzled her hand. "You're going to be fine."

Ella settled the pony into her fresh, clean stable. "We're going to be fine!" she told herself, trying to forget the morning's events. "Dad will sort things out with Mr. and Mrs. Brooks. The forecast will be wrong, and tomorrow will be a beautiful sunny day. There'll be a huge crowd! And Jake Adams will be the star attraction!"

"I wouldn't count on it if I were you." Caleb had wandered into the stable. There was a deep frown on his face.

"Uh-oh, it's Mr. Grumpy!" Ella told Rosie. "Seems like he's in a bad mood. Don't take any notice."

Caleb sniffed and went to pet Apache.

"He gets like this," Ella explained brightly, as if Rosie understood every word. "Something probably went wrong with the website. Maybe he can't download a picture or maybe he deleted something by mistake."

Caleb's mood darkened. "Cut it out, Ella!"

She made a face behind his back. Then she felt bad for teasing him. "Okay, okay, I'm sorry. Is something really wrong?"

He sighed, turned away, and then
strode back toward her. "We got a
message from Jake Adams," he told her.

Ella's heart did a little flip, and
seemed to stop and then start again.
"Saying what?" she whispered.

Caleb looked her in the eyes and gave
her the bad news. "Saying he can't
come to the anniversary celebration," he
reported. "Something happened. He had
to leave."

Ella gasped. She shook her head in
disbelief.

"It's true," Caleb insisted. "It's all off.
Jake won't be here tomorrow. *Finito.* End
of story. *Kaput.*"

35

Chapter Four

"Jake didn't give a reason," Caleb insisted, shaking his head in disbelief. "He just said he had to leave. I can show you the email if you want. I tried to send him a reply but it just bounced back."

"No reasons and no apology?" Dad remarked. He'd come home early to help with the preparations. "I'm really surprised. I had Jake Adams down as a decent sort of guy."

"Me, too," Caleb said gloomily.

"So now we have no celebrity." Ella's mom sighed. "And it's too late either to find someone else or to let people know."

Ella sat without saying a word. Mrs. Brooks was on the warpath, it was going to rain, and now Jake couldn't come. Their big day lay in ruins.

"Maybe we should cancel the whole thing," Caleb muttered.

"No, no, we have to go ahead," his dad argued. "Keep in mind that our main goal is to find new homes for our animals. It's a huge shame that Jake's not coming, but people will still be able to look around the place, and we can still match up pets with new owners just the same."

"But it won't be the same!" Caleb insisted. "Everyone will be disappointed.

What am I going to tell George when he shows up expecting to get Jake's autograph?"

"Dad's right," Mom cut in. "We have to go ahead. Mark, do you want to go next door to calm Linda down, or should I?"

Ella's dad got up from the table and headed for the door. "I'll do it."

Ella turned to Caleb, who was still moping. "I want to look at Jake's email. Can I use the computer in your room?"

"Feel free." He followed Ella upstairs and quickly went online.

Ella frowned as she read the message.

```
From: Jake Adams
To: Animal Magic

Subject: Anniversary Celebration

Message: Can't come tomorrow.
         Have to leave. Jake.
```

She pressed the reply button and wrote, "Can Marietta still make it?" Then she pressed send. The message stayed in the outbox, then came back unsent.

"See?" Caleb sighed. "Anyway, what's the point?"

"Marietta would be better than no one," Ella replied. "She gets in all the celebrity magazines. She's always going to parties with famous people."

Caleb nodded. "But if we can't send an email, we're stuck."

Ella frowned. She wasn't giving up that easily. She headed downstairs and into the yard. "No, we're not!"

"What are you doing? Where are you going?" Caleb watched her grab her bike.

"I'm doing what people did before they had email. I'm going to ride out to Crystal Park Manor and speak to Marietta!"

Caleb's mouth dropped open. "Hey, wait! No, hang on!" He ran for his own bike and followed Ella onto Main Street.

"I'm coming, too!" Caleb called after her. "Ella, wait for me!"

Chapter Five

"O-o-oh, wow!" Caleb stopped beside Ella at the gates of Crystal Park Manor. Caleb had never seen the house before, even though he knew, like all the rest of the world, that Jake Adams and his girlfriend had recently moved in.

The soccer star's home was fairytale stuff—a massive old house with a long, tree-lined drive. It had square towers and big stone pillars. "Where's the swimming pool?" he asked.

"Around the back," Ella told him. "Marietta gave Dad and me a quick tour when we came to drop Charlie off."

Caleb got off his bike and propped it against the wall. He inspected the fancy iron gates. "These gates are electronic and they're locked. What do we do now?"

"Press that button and speak into the microphone thing?" Ella suggested.

Caleb pressed, but nothing happened. "Looks like there's no one home. Come on, let's go."

"We're not going to give up that easily!" Starting to pedal again, Ella made her way cautiously along the road until she came to a narrow side lane. "Come on!" she called.

The lane was rough and overgrown, but as Ella expected, it led down the side of

Crystal Park Manor. A little way down she spotted what she'd been looking for.

"Look, there's a gate into the yard." Leaving her bike in some long grass, Ella went ahead and tested the handle. "And this one's open!"

She pushed the gate and stepped onto the soccer idol's smooth green lawn.

"Whoa, we could be in trouble here!" Caleb pointed out. "This is trespassing."

Ella rolled her eyes. "I've been here before, remember? Marietta and Jake know me!"

Swallowing hard, Caleb followed his sister across the wide lawn, and then past a bright blue open-air pool.

Ella led the way toward a door at the back of the old manor house and rang the bell. Once again, there was no answer.

"Look, they've both left," Caleb insisted, turning to go. "We're wasting our time. Come on."

"They can't have both left," Ella protested. "What about Charlie?"

Caleb shrugged. "What about Charlie?"

Ella peered through the glass panels of the door. "He only just came here. They wouldn't leave him home alone."

"Maybe a neighbor is taking care of him. Come on, Ella, let's go!"

As Ella continued peering into the house, Caleb turned to see a small orange and white shape peek out from behind one of the large flowerpots beside the door.

"Uh-oh!" he said, watching the fluffy kitten emerge from his hiding place. Charlie had a cute little face and two white paws. "You shouldn't be outside by yourself!"

Ella spun around and spotted him. "So much for him being taken care of by a neighbor!" she muttered.

Scared and alone, the kitten began to run. He darted between more plant pots, charging this way and that toward the swimming pool.

"Oh, no!" Ella saw the danger and began to run after Charlie. She tried to cut him off, but he scooted between her feet, under a poolside chair and … splash, straight into the deep end of the pool!

Ella cried out as she watched poor little Charlie sink beneath the surface.

A split second later Caleb was racing toward the pool. He jumped in after the kitten, fully clothed.

Ella squeezed her eyes shut, hardly

daring to watch. When she opened
them again, Caleb had already caught
Charlie and was pulling him back to the
surface, holding him clear of the water.

"Here!" he yelled at Ella. "Grab him!"

She knelt and leaned out over the
water to take the dripping kitten. "Are
you okay?" she asked Caleb.

"Yes, don't worry about me. How's Charlie?"

The kitten meowed and shivered in her arms. Ella took off her jacket and quickly wrapped him in it. "He'll be fine."

As Caleb hauled himself out of the pool, Ella rubbed the kitten dry. She felt his rough little tongue lick her hand and saw his bright green eyes peer out from the folds of her jacket. "Don't worry," she whispered. "You're safe now."

"And I'm dripping wet!" Caleb groaned, taking off a sneaker and dumping out the water from it. "Honestly, Ella, I wish we'd never come!"

"Hush!" she told Charlie as he meowed and licked. "Of course it's a good thing we came."

"Yeah, so we could scare the poor little thing and make him jump into the pool! Like that was a really good thing!"

Ella sighed. "Look, Caleb. There's no cat flap. If we hadn't come, Charlie would have been locked out and left all by himself. He could have fallen into the pool at any time, and there would have been no one around to rescue him!"

"Yeah, I see what you mean," Caleb grunted, putting his shoes back on.

"How could Jake and Marietta leave him?" Ella said. "What were they thinking?" She made up her mind about what they had to do and began to head back the way they'd come. "We can't leave Charlie here. We'll have to take him back to Animal Magic!"

Shaking his head like a dog drying itself, Caleb ran after her. "Hang on! Let's just think this through."

But Ella didn't hesitate. "I'm not leaving Charlie home alone!" she insisted. "I don't care who Jake Adams is, or what he says. Charlie is coming back with us!"

Chapter Six

"So now we have the mystery of the vanishing soccer star and the home-alone kitten on our hands." Ella's mom had taken Rosie's temperature and checked her pulse. Both were back to normal, and the pony stood comfortably in her stall.

"How could we get it so wrong in the first place?" Ella wondered. She stood with Charlie snuggled inside her jacket, fast asleep.

She and Caleb had carried Charlie back from Crystal Park Manor and told their mom what had happened. Mom had sent Caleb inside the house to change into dry clothes.

"We followed our Animal Magic rules and we all thought Jake and Marietta were the perfect owners for the perfect pet!" Ella pointed out.

"We can't be right one hundred percent of the time," her mom said. "Hello again, little cutie," she said, tickling Charlie's chin. "I hear you've just used up one of your nine lives!"

"But Mom, you said Jake seemed to love cats," Ella reminded her. "Marietta, too—you said she wanted to take them all home!"

Taking Charlie from Ella, Mom

led the way out of the stables toward
the cat unit. "But people sometimes
promise things, then don't act on their
promises. They meant well at the time,
I suppose."

Mom popped Charlie into the kitten
unit that housed Candy, Snap, and
Pixie. "Say hello to your brother!" she
said with a smile.

The boldest of the kittens was Snap,
and he came forward to greet Charlie by
sniffing and raising his front paw.

Charlie meowed and backed away, straight into Snap. Then Pixie pounced on Charlie and began to play-fight.

"Pixie loves you, really!" Ella laughed, as Charlie entered into the rough and tumble.

"The question is, are we going to let Charlie go back to Crystal Park Manor?"

"No way!"

Mom gave Ella a serious look. "Not even if there's a good explanation?"

"Nope." As far as Ella was concerned, Jake and Marietta could never come up with a good enough reason to explain why they'd abandoned Charlie.

Before Mom could reply, they heard Dad calling for her from the yard.

"In the cat unit!" Mom called back.

Ella's dad joined them. "I just got

back from the Brookses' place," he muttered, a dazed look on his face.

"That was a long visit," said Ella.

Dad scratched his head. "Yeah, I don't know what happened. I went to explain about our anniversary celebration, and before I knew it, Linda Brooks was offering me coffee, and Jason was going through all his old soccer scrapbooks with me."

"How come?" Ella asked.

"Does this mean that peace has broken out?" Mom said at the same time.

"Linda has found out about Jake Adams being our star guest tomorrow," Dad explained. "Don't ask me how. Anyway, she told Jason, and it turns out Jason is a huge fan."

"But—" Ella tried to interrupt.

Her dad cut her off. "I know, but listen. As soon as Jason heard, he convinced Linda that our anniversary celebration was a good thing because it would mean many of our pets would find new homes, and this place would be a lot less crowded and noisy. Which means it'll be quieter for them in the near future."

"But—" Ella tried again.

"I know, can you believe it?" He sighed and spread his hands, palms upward. "They said they might even drop by tomorrow to see Jake."

"But Jake isn't coming!" Ella pointed out at last.

Her dad frowned. "I know. But I couldn't get a word in edgewise, and in the end I just didn't have the heart to tell them!"

Chapter Seven

"So what's going to happen to you?"
Ella asked Charlie when she went to
visit him later that evening.

Charlie was snuggled up next to
Candy, curled into a soft ball with his
white front paws tucked under his chin.
The tip of his orange tail twitched as
Ella leaned in to pet him.

"It's okay, I won't disturb you," she
whispered. "I'm just wondering what'll
happen now. I hope Mom doesn't let

you go back to Jake's place. I hope she lets us find you someone new."

Charlie let his top lids sink down over his bright green eyes and he fell asleep.

"But if they do send you back, you have to promise not to go for another swim!" Ella went on. "Remember, water and cats don't mix!"

Next to Charlie, Snap opened his mouth and yawned. Over in the corner of the unit, Pixie and Candy were already fast asleep.

"Water—nasty, cold, wet stuff!" Ella insisted. "Brrr!"

Charlie opened one eye, and then closed it again.

"Okay, I'll let you get some sleep." Ella smiled, giving him one last pet. There were so many problems to solve and questions hanging over the kitten's future, but now it was late and everyone was tired. "Good night, Snap," she said. "Good night, Charlie. Sleep well!"

"Sleep well, Ella," her dad said as he'd turned off the light.

Ella lay on her back, staring up at the ceiling. She wasn't sleepy at all— her head was too busy worrying about Charlie and wondering why his new owners had let him down.

I don't get it! she thought over and over. *Why would anyone adopt a kitten and then leave him home alone?*

She remembered poor little Charlie hiding among the big plant pots at Crystal Park Manor.

He must have been hungry! she thought. *And lonely and scared!*

When she finally drifted off, her sleep was full of dreams about dark, glittering swimming pools and empty houses that had long, creepy hallways with creaking doors and spooky, whispering voices.

"Oh!" Ella woke up from her nightmare. She pulled her quilt tightly around her shoulders, gradually realizing that daylight was already filtering through her curtains. "Phew!" She breathed a sigh of relief.

Throwing back her sheets, she went to open the curtains. "Rain!" she groaned, peering out. The yard was covered in puddles, the slate roof of the clinic was shiny, and water trickled along the gutters. "What a rotten start to our anniversary celebration!"

Ella got dressed and went downstairs.
She was halfway through her bowl of
cereal before she looked at the clock
and saw that it was only ten to six. No
wonder no one else was up.

Okay, so what do I do now? she wondered.
*Go back to bed? No, I know—I could send one
last email to Jake! Surely it's worth a try.*

She flung on her rain boots and
waterproof jacket and trotted across the
yard to the clinic, where Joel Allerton
was just finishing his night shift.

"What are you doing up so early?" Joel asked Ella. He yawned and ran his hand through his hair, checking off medicines on the shelf against a list of stock on the computer screen.

"Couldn't sleep," she said, logging onto the computer next to Joel's. "Just wanted to send an email!"

Ella brought up the message from Jake and the one that she and Caleb had tried and failed to send. "Can Marietta still make it?" She tried again. Once more the mail server sent it back.

"No good," Ella muttered. She was over her disappointment and starting to get angry. "How come people you trust let you down?" she asked Joel.

"Which people?" Joel glanced at the screen. "Oh, you mean our local soccer

62

legend? I guess something important came up for him."

"This is important!" Ella insisted, pointing at one of the anniversary celebration fliers. "And so is adopting a kitten!"

"Ah, you mean Charlie." Joel had been keeping an eye on the orange-and-white kitten all night to make sure he'd settled back in with his brother and sisters. "I'm with you on that one!"

Ella nodded. "I want to know what's going on."

"We know what's going on," Joel pointed out. "Some big-shot sports star makes a spur-of-the-moment decision to adopt a cute kitten for his girlfriend. But a few days later she's bored with kitty and they get invited to a friend's

Spanish villa or whatever. Then it's bye-bye, Charlie, hello sunbathing!"

"It's so not fair!" Ella muttered, feeling even more angry. She jumped up from the computer, making her own on-the-spot decision. "If you see Mom and Dad, tell them I won't be long."

Joel glanced up from his monitor. "Why? Where are you going?"

"Out!" Ella announced. "Back to Crystal Park Manor, to find out why Jake and Marietta abandoned Charlie!"

Ella cycled through the rain. Drops fell from her helmet onto her cold cheeks. Her jeans were soon soaked through.

No traffic, she thought with relief, splashing through puddles. She noticed

the wet cows in the fields, and a sad-
looking horse poking its head over one
of the bushes as she sped along the
country road leading to the mansion.

But as she approached the wide gates,
the morning silence was broken by the
loud revving of a car's engine.

Ella braked and pulled into the grass.
The sound of the engine grew louder
and a small blue car shot out from
Crystal Park Manor Drive and headed
her way with a roar and squeal of tires.

"Hey!" Ella cried, catching sight of a
dark-haired woman at the wheel.

The woman sped past without
seeming to notice her.

"Charming!" Ella muttered, her heart
in her mouth. "And she didn't even bother
to press the button and close the gates!"

As the sports car disappeared down the road, Ella saw her chance and rode down the drive toward the mansion.

In the early morning rain the old house looked dark and spooky, just like the haunted house in her dream. Ella could easily picture ghosts floating down hallways and gazing down at her from the rafters.

Get a grip! she told herself as she approached the wide front door. *And who was that woman in the blue car? It wasn't Marietta. And the car wasn't here when Caleb and I came yesterday. What on earth is going on?*

Speaking of cars, Ella thought it would be a good idea to check the garage. "If Jake and Marietta are away, their cars won't be here," she said out loud, skirting down the side of the house to peer through the small windows of an old stable block. To her surprise there were two cars parked inside. *Maybe they're back!* she thought.

She walked up to the front of the house and found the doorbell. *What now?* Ella wondered. Should she press it, or was it way too early to disturb Jake?

Her finger hovered over the buzzer.

Then her gaze was drawn to a soggy piece of paper on the rain-spattered step. Ella stooped to pick it up. It was a smudged, hastily written message.

Dear Bobbie,

Please feed Charlie. Food is on the kitchen table. Leave him in laundry room with clean litter box. Close door behind you. Back Sunday.

Love Marietta x

Ella's eyes opened wide. She smoothed the note and read it again.

So Jake and Marietta hadn't dumped Charlie after all. They'd had a plan to have him taken care of by someone named Bobbie. But it had all gone wrong.

Bobbie hadn't shown up when he was supposed to, and now Charlie was back at the rescue center. Which left two big questions in Ella's mind. Who was the woman in the blue sports car? And why was she in such a hurry to get away?

Chapter Eight

In spite of Ella's doubts, by nine o'clock, the yard at Animal Magic was buzzing with activity. Ella watched people come and go. She had said nothing about her early morning visit to the mansion or the mysterious blue car that had shot out of the driveway. She was still thinking about it when she saw a Land Rover splash through the puddles and enter the yard. She waved and ran to greet her grandpa.

"Did you come to help?" she asked,

as Jim Harrison climbed out of the car. Ella grabbed him by the hand, steering him past the biggest puddles.

"You bet!" he grinned.

"What about Gro-well?"

Ella and Caleb's grandpa ran a small garden center on the outskirts of town. You never saw him without his green gardening vest and a pair of pruning shears stuffed in his pocket.

"I left Thomas in charge. He's been working for me long enough. I figure he can manage by himself for one day." Still smiling, he waved at Dad and Caleb. "When does the great man arrive?" he yelled. "Jake Adams is a real crowd-puller. Are you ready for the rush?"

Ella bit her lip. "Grandpa, didn't Dad tell you?"

"Tell me what?" Grandpa put on his flat cap and zipped up his vest.

Ella broke the news bluntly. "Jake Adams isn't coming. He backed out at the last minute."

"Wow!" a voice from next door gasped. Annie's head appeared over the bushes. "Are you serious?"

Ella's shoulders sagged. "Jake can't come," she admitted. "Anyway, what are you doing, Annie? You're not supposed to listen to other people's conversations!"

"I can't help it if I happen to be in my yard!" Annie protested weakly.

"I'll leave you two to sort it out," Grandpa said, shaking his head and looking disappointed as he went off to find a job to do.

"You're never in your yard!" Ella said to Annie. "Especially when it's raining. You hate getting your hair wet!"

Annie ignored her. "What happened to Jake?"

"Don't ask me." Wiping the rain from her face, Ella realized it was no use being upset with Annie. "I'm sorry," she mumbled. "I know it's not your fault."

"No worries," Annie replied.

"Don't tell your dad," Ella pleaded. "He'll think we made it up—the stuff about Jake coming—just to stop your mom from complaining about us."

Annie nodded. "Okay, I won't say anything. But he's going to find out soon any—"

At that moment there was a blast from a car horn in the driveway next door, and the sound of a car's tires squealing to a halt.

"Oops!" Annie turned in time to see her mom stop sharply at the end of their driveway.

Out of the corner of her eye, Ella saw a second car on Main Street. The driver jammed on the brakes. "That was close!" she breathed.

The second car swerved, then crunched into the lamppost outside Annie's house.

"Ouch!" Ella grimaced. She saw Caleb sprint across the yard toward the road and she quickly followed. By the time they reached the gate, Linda Brooks was already out of her car and standing on the pavement, while a dark-haired woman stepped shakily out of her small blue car.

"What do you think you're doing?" Linda shrieked. "This is a 30-mile-per-hour zone! You must have been doing at least 50!"

"Are you okay?" Caleb asked the woman, noticing her front bumper bent around the lamppost and a hiss of steam emerging from under the hood.

Soon other people came running, including Ella's dad, who quickly took control. "Caleb, please go down the street and try to warn drivers that there's been an accident. Get them to slow down."

75

Caleb nodded and hurried off.

Ella stayed at her dad's side. She'd recognized the crashed car—it was the same one that she'd seen at Crystal Park Manor.

"Linda, are you okay?" Dad asked. Then he turned back to the other driver. "You've probably had a bit of a shock. Would you like to come inside while we sort all of this out?"

"Don't touch the car!" Linda insisted. "I'm going to call the police. They'll have to measure braking distances before it gets towed away."

Sighing, Dad led the woman toward the house.

"I wasn't breaking the speed limit." The young woman spoke for the first time. "Your neighbor shot out from her driveway without looking. I had to swerve to avoid her."

Hearing this, Ella frowned. She'd seen how fast the woman had come out of the driveway at Crystal Park Manor a few hours earlier. But she didn't say anything.

"I'm so sorry to bother you," the woman went on, sitting down in the kitchen and accepting a cup of tea.

"It looks like you're very busy."

"No problem," Dad assured her. "Stay here. Ella will keep you company. I'll go outside and wait for the police."

Nodding, the woman took a deep breath and sipped her tea.

"Did you come to Crystal Park for a reason?" Ella asked carefully, her curiosity bubbling over in spite of the shock of the accident.

The woman looked pale and worried. She was young, with long, glossy brown hair. "I went to my sister's house, but she wasn't home."

"Where?"

The woman glanced cautiously at Ella. "It doesn't matter. Never mind."

She's hiding something! Ella thought. But there was no time to ask more

questions, because her dad reappeared
with a police officer who immediately
asked to see the woman's driver's license.

"Roberta Jarvis," the policeman said,
reading the name on the license and
writing it down. "Now, Miss Jarvis, how
fast were you driving at the time of the
accident?"

"Mom's gone crazy!" Annie reported to
Ella an hour after the policeman had left.
"She's denying coming out of the driveway
without looking, and she's saying that
Roberta Jarvis was doing 50!"

"Well, I heard Roberta tell the police
that she was under the speed limit," Ella
replied.

"Ella, can you check the hay in Rosie's
and Apache's nets?" her mom called
from the clinic door.

Ella started toward the stables. "See
you later," she told Annie. As she
crossed the yard, her dad appeared at
the back door with Roberta. He hurried
over to Grandpa, who was helping
Caleb put up some bunting.

"Dad, could you please give Roberta a lift?" he asked. "Her car's not driveable, and she needs to get home."

"Of course." Grandpa smiled kindly at the pale young woman. "Where's home?"

"In Hudson," she explained with a hesitant smile. "I'm sorry to put you to all this trouble."

"No problem," he assured her. "It's only a couple of miles."

Hearing this, Ella dashed on into the stable to check on the ponies' feed, and then hurried back out. "I'll go with Grandpa," she told her dad.

Ella climbed into the backseat of the Land Rover with Roberta. Grandpa pulled out of the yard and switched on the radio.

"I'm sorry!" Roberta said again, seemingly on the verge of tears.

Grandpa drove on past her smashed car without replying.

"He didn't hear you. He's a little deaf," Ella explained. "I saw you earlier," she said quietly.

Roberta shot her a worried look. "Where?"

Ella looked her in the eye. "At Jake Adams's place."

Roberta frowned. "Why were you snooping around there?"

"I was going to ask you that," Ella retorted. "Come on, you tell me first."

"I was looking for a cat," Roberta sighed. "A kitten actually. It belongs to my sister."

It was Ella's turn to frown.

"Marietta?"

Roberta nodded. "She and Jake had to go out of town all of a sudden."

"Marietta's your sister?"

"Yes. She asked me to take care of her kitten. But it escaped from the house and ran off."

Hang on a second! Ella tried to fit the pieces together. True, Marietta and Jake had had a sudden change of plan. But hadn't she found the note addressed to a man named Bobbie, asking him to take care of Charlie? That didn't make sense!

"I came to the mansion at lunchtime yesterday," Roberta went on. "I only opened the back door a little way, but Charlie shot out between my legs and vanished!"

"Charlie!" Ella echoed. *Roberta—Bobbie. Bobbie's not a man—she's a woman!*

"I came back twice in the afternoon to look for him, but he never showed up," Bobbie explained. "And I got up early this morning and came over first thing. And again just after nine. Still no luck. Poor little Charlie has vanished into thin air. I have no idea what I'm going to tell Marietta when she gets back!"

Chapter Nine

"Grandpa, turn around!" Ella cried. She leaned forward and tapped his shoulder. "Take us back to Animal Magic, please!"

"Make up your mind," her grandpa grumbled.

Bobbie turned to Ella with a puzzled look. "What's up? Why are we going back?"

Ella took a deep breath. Suddenly everything looked different. "There's been a big mistake!" she gasped. "Caleb and I … we thought … well, anyway, you'll soon see!"

Grandpa turned the car around and set off back to the rescue center.

"My brother and I wanted to find out why Jake had changed his mind about coming to our anniversary celebration," Ella told Bobbie. "He promised to be here, but then he backed out. That's why we went to Crystal Park Manor yesterday afternoon."

"Uh-oh, Ella. What have you been up to this time?" her grandpa asked.

"The house was empty … and, well … we thought poor little Charlie had been left without anyone to take care of him."

Bobbie nodded. "Okay, I get it. But

actually I was the one who messed up in the first place by letting Charlie escape. He ran off and I couldn't get him to come back. I didn't know what to do!"

"Here we are, girls!" Grandpa announced, pulling into the yard at Animal Magic.

"Come on!" Ella urged Marietta's confused sister. She led her toward the cat unit and headed straight for the cage containing Charlie and his brothers and sister. "Excuse me," she said to a couple of visitors who were gazing at the adorable litter. Then she leaned over and picked up the snuggly, fluffy orange-and-white kitten.

"Charlie!" Bobbie gasped in total amazement. "Oh, Charlie, there you are! Thank goodness!"

"Am I in trouble?" Ella asked her mom as Bobbie cuddled Charlie.

Immediately, Bobbie stood up for Ella. "Oh, please don't be upset with her! She did what she thought was best. And she saved Charlie from drowning, remember?"

"Actually, that was Caleb," Ella admitted. Her brother hovered in the background, ready to jump in if things turned ugly.

"You're right, Bobbie." Mom nodded. She reached out and petted Charlie. "All's well that ends well."

Phew! Ella relaxed and Caleb sidled up, smiling, hands in his pockets.

"Thank you so much!" Bobbie said to

him. "You saved Charlie's life!"

"Do you happen to know why Jake had to cancel?" Caleb asked. "We're going to look really silly when Mom has to make the announcement that he won't be here after all."

"I'm sorry. I really don't know." Bobbie held on tight to Charlie and walked with Mom, Ella, and Caleb out into the yard. There was a distant roll of thunder and heavy splashes of rain. Wet visitors scuttled from the kennels to the cat unit, and on into the converted barn that held the rabbits and guinea pigs. "I can't help you. I wish I could."

"Didn't Marietta tell you?" Ella persisted.

Bobbie shook her head. "Can I please call a taxi? I have to get Charlie back to Crystal Park Manor. And this time, I'll make sure he doesn't get out of the house!"

Ella's grandpa overheard and stepped forward. "No need for a taxi. I'll bring you there. As long as you don't change your mind again halfway!"

Soon Ella, Bobbie, and Charlie were back in the Land Rover with Grandpa, heading for the mansion.

"So Marietta didn't explain where she and Jake were going?" Ella prompted again.

"I thought it was a little weird at the time," Bobbie confessed. "Marietta seemed upset when she called me and told me they had to leave so suddenly. She wouldn't explain—just asked me to take care of Charlie."

There was a short silence, and then Bobbie went on. "If you ask me, it had to do with the Angela Nixon fiasco."

"Who's she?" Ella asked.

"She is—no, she was until recently—Jake's personal assistant. She lived at the mansion with Jake and Marietta.

But my sister found out on Thursday that Angela had been incorrectly reporting her expenses, and Jake fired her on the spot."

"But what does that have to do with Jake having to leave unexpectedly?" Ella didn't see it, and Bobbie had no real answers for her.

"I don't know—just a feeling," she said.

They lapsed into silence again as Grandpa turned into the driveway of Crystal Park Manor and drove slowly through the still-open gates toward the big old house.

"Home again!" Bobbie said to Charlie as she unlocked the front door.

The orange-and-white kitten sniffed

and wriggled. Bobbie put him down
gently and watched him stick his pointy
tail straight up in the air and pad
carefully across the polished floor.

Meow! Charlie said, heading for the
kitchen.

"Maybe he's hungry," Bobbie
wondered, inviting Ella and Grandpa
into the house.

"More like thirsty." Ella knew that the kittens had already been fed. She smiled to see Charlie lap greedily at the saucer of water that Bobbie put down.

Bobbie's phone rang, and she hurried to answer it.

"Marietta!" she said, walking quickly out of the kitchen and into the hall.

Ella couldn't hear what was being said, but she could tell that Bobbie sounded surprised. "Maybe now we'll find out what happened to Jake," she said glumly to her grandpa. They waited for Bobbie to come back.

"I knew it!" Bobbie frowned, pacing up and down the big kitchen. "It is Angela Nixon! I knew she was bad news. Not only does she deliberately crash Jake's computer when she finds out she's been sacked, she sends him off for a big meeting with the team's boss that hasn't even been arranged!"

Ella's grandpa whistled gently. "Not Mark Moorcroft himself!"

Bobbie took a deep breath. "Yes, the big boss. Apparently Angela said Moorcroft needed to talk to Jake about renewing his contract. She made it seem like his future at the club was in doubt and got him to drive all the way to Moorcroft's office, only to find out that there was no meeting after all. Moorcroft didn't show up, and it turns out that he's on vacation with his family in Florida."

"Wow! That's mean!" Suddenly a new thought flashed into her head. "Where are Jake and Marietta right now?"

"On their way home."

"On their way home!" Ella echoed. "Wow, Bobbie, that's cool! Did they say…? I mean, can you call them back? Find out if…."

Grandpa stepped in with a smile to help Ella out. "I think what my excited granddaughter is trying to say is, will you ask Jake if he'll be back in time to make an appearance at our anniversary celebration?"

Chapter Ten

It was after one o'clock when Ella and her grandfather arrived back at Animal Magic.

"Remember, don't say anything to your mom and dad about Jake," Grandpa said, holding the car door open for Ella to jump out.

At the mansion, Bobbie had promised Ella that she would call Marietta back, but she had warned them not to place too much hope on the celebrity couple being back in time.

"I wouldn't want you to be disappointed all over again," she'd told Ella.

Even so, Ella's brown eyes were sparkling with excitement, and it was almost more than she could bear. *Jake, be here!* she begged silently. *Please be here! Everyone's still expecting you. Don't let us down!*

Meanwhile, visitors crowded into the yard. There was a buzz of conversation as people went from kennels to cat unit to stables, and all the talk was about the soccer superstar.

"Where's Jake Adams…? He's not due until two…. It's good of him to support an animal rescue center…. I'll bet he's a really nice guy!"

Ella followed a family into the stables

where Rosie and Apache munched hay.

"Look at the little brown pony, Mom!" the girl cried. "It says on the label that her name's Rosie. How sweet is she!"

"Gorgeous," the woman agreed. "I had a pony just like her when I was your age."

Ella grinned and crossed her fingers. She moved onto the dog kennels, where a young couple were looking at Beckett.

"Beautiful!" the woman sighed, bending down to the great dane's eye level. "These dogs have gentle natures in spite of their size. Oh, Ben, wouldn't it be great to give Beckett a home!"

Fingers crossed! Ella smiled and went on, past Pepper's and Bruno's kennels. This could work out perfectly—if only

Jake Adams could make it here in time!

"Hello, Ella!" Outside in the yard once more, she heard Annie's dad call her name. "Where's Jake? Is he here yet?"

Ella took a deep breath and held back her answer. "I don't know. Better ask Mom!" *Phew!* She breathed a sigh of relief as Jason continued on. Then she spotted Annie hanging around by herself outside the cat unit.

"What a day!" Ella said, starting to tell Annie about Charlie. "He hadn't been left home alone after all! You know the woman in the blue sports car who ran into the lamppost? Well, it turns out she—"

"Stop!" Annie pleaded. She shook her head unhappily. "Didn't Dad tell you?"

"No. What?"

"About the accident. The police got back in touch. It looks like the woman in the blue car—"

"Bobbie," Ella interrupted. "Short for Roberta."

"Yes, whatever. Well, it looks like she was going less than 30 miles an hour after all. And it was Mom who backed out without looking."

"Whoa!" Ella stared at her friend.

"I know. Mom's so upset. I'm sure she'll have to apologize to Roberta." Annie predicted that the next few days at home were going to be tough. "We don't know yet if the police will charge her."

"Wow!" Ella took a step back. "Hey, look, the sun just came out!"

"Just in time for me to make my announcement about Jake," Ella's mom muttered as she passed by with Dad. "I'm not looking forward to this!"

Ella glanced at her watch and saw that it was almost two o'clock. *Okay, I guess it was too much to hope for*, she told herself. *It would have been like a little*

*piece of pure magic if Jake had shown up
in time!*

Still expecting the soccer star to
appear on the scene, the crowd of
visitors gathered around. Ella spotted
Jason Brooks and Caleb's friend, George
Stevens, along with a hundred other
eager faces. This was the moment they
had all been waiting for. "Oh, no, poor
Mom having to tell them!" she groaned.

"Ladies and gentlemen, thank you for
coming," Mom began. "We're glad that
so many of you have come out to see the
work we do here at Animal Magic."

Mom smiled at the excited crowd and
took a deep breath. "Unfortunately…."

But just as Ella hung her head, dreading
her mom's next words, a car drove slowly
into the yard and came to a stop.

All heads turned. The driver's door opened and Jake Adams stepped out.

A big cheer went up as everyone turned to greet the great man. Ella's mom stood outside the clinic door, wearing a look of stunned surprise.

Thank you! Ella clasped her hands together and jumped up and down.

"Jake, can I have your autograph! …
Jake, write on this shirt! … Jake, you're
the best player the team has ever had!"

As the crowd swamped Jake Adams,
Bobbie got out of the car with Marietta.
They saw Ella and waved her to come
over. "You're a star!" Marietta told her.
"Bobbie has told me everything you and
Caleb did for Charlie."

Ella grinned and blushed, unable to
think of anything to say. In any case,
she saw that Jake had finally escaped
from his fans and was standing by the
clinic door, ready to make a speech. He
looked shy and uncomfortable, waiting
for the noise to die down.

"I just want to say what a great place
this is," Jake began. "Heidi and her
team are doing a wonderful job, and

all the animals that end up at Animal Magic are extremely lucky. I just wish there were more centers like this."

"Yeah!" Ella said, along with a lot of other people in the crowd.

"They need your support," Jake went on, "so now that you're here, why don't you stick around and adopt a pet, like we did? Go on, do it. Show that you care!"

"Cool!" Ella cried, clapping loudly, and then cheering as Jake disappeared inside the clinic. "We love you, Jake!" she yelled. "We love you. We really do!"

Chapter Eleven

"We've found new homes for three rabbits and two guinea pigs," Dad said.

Caleb clicked his mouse and brought up the details on the Animal Magic website. He put check marks next to pictures of the pets who had been adopted.

"We also found families for six dogs, including Pepper, Bruno, and Beckett," Joel reported.

"Wonderful!" Ella nodded happily.

"And what about Rosie?"

"Maybe," Joel said. "It depends what we find out about her current owners when they come back from their vacation. If it turns out the way we want it to, she'll go to the Boswells, because they can offer her a cozy new home."

"Cool." Their anniversary celebration had worked out perfectly—better than even Ella could have hoped.

"Best of all, we matched nine cats with new owners," Mom told everyone. "Pixie and Candy both went to a very nice retired lady in town."

"Oh, poor Snap," Ella whispered. "That means he's still here by himself."

Caleb clicked and checked a box. "That's 21 animals altogether," he said.

"How cool is that!"

"Twenty-two!" a voice said, and they all turned to see Bobbie, Jake, and Marietta standing in the doorway.

Caleb counted again. "Three plus two plus six plus one plus nine. That makes 21," he insisted.

But Bobbie came forward holding a squirming tabby kitten in her hands. "I'd like to adopt Snap," she said. "If you think I'll be a good owner, that is."

Mom looked at Ella. "What do you think?"

Ella went up to Bobbie and took Snap from her. She cuddled him close. "I think you'll be perfect!" she said to Bobbie. She was sure Bobbie would take care of him and feed him and keep him safe. "You know Dad found him in an air vent behind a factory?"

Bobbie, Jake, and Marietta listened to the whole story as Ella took Snap out into the warm sunshine.

"Dad works for a package delivery company. He was in the factory parking lot when he heard a meowing sound coming from the air vent, so he went to take a look...."

Caleb, Mom, and Dad stood in the doorway watching Ella chat with their guests.

"So cool!" Caleb sighed, staring at
Jake and suffering from a serious case of
hero worship.

"A good day!" Mom said, bringing out
a cardboard pet carrier for the kitten.
Animal Magic had done its job.

Ella put Snap into the carrier and
took him over to Jake's car.

"He's been microchipped, and he's
had his shots," Ella assured Bobbie. "No
need to worry about that."

As Jake started the engine, Marietta
leaned out the window. "Thanks, Ella!"

Ella nodded and smiled. Her dad
came to join her, and he put his arm
around her shoulder.

"Give me a shout anytime you need
me," Jake told him as he put the car
into gear.

As they watched the soccer star leave the yard, Ella looked up at her dad. "Okay," she said, her eyes sparkling, a grin spreading across her face from ear to ear. "When is our next Animal Magic anniversary celebration?!"